The author of this book does not dispense or prescribe any technique. The
author intends to offer information of a general nature to help a young person
in their quest for reading and enhanced literacy. In the event you use any of the
information in this book for yourself, which is your constitutional right, the
author or publisher assume no responsibility for your actions.

Illustrator – Carol Ada
Editor – Dr. James E. Bruce, Jr.
Book Coach – The Self Publishing Maven
Interior Design – Istvan Szabo, Ifj., Sapphire Guardian International

ISBN13: 978-1-7323622-0-8
LCCN 2018905970

Printed in the United States of America

For our children
&
Andrew, you are my greatest blessing

Table of Contents

Life for an eleven-year-old girl is stressful.
We experience so much with our families, friends, and classmates.
Having the right people in your corner can make the journey amazing and worthwhile. Come along with me and let's see how it turns out.

Chapter 1
New York... New Life

Have you been on an airplane before? Well, it's my second time. The first time was last year when my family and I went to Seattle to visit my Aunt Pam for Thanksgiving. The flight from Memphis to Seattle was extremely long. I think it was about four hours, but it felt a lot longer. I had books, music, and games to keep me entertained, and still, I was going out of my mind. I felt confined to one space; it was so dreadful. I wished the Space Needle could have popped my balloon of frustration and impatience.

This time, we are flying to New York City a.k.a The Big Apple a.k.a The Concrete Jungle. I still need to find out what all of these nicknames really mean, especially if this is supposed to be my new home. Dad claims "If you can make it here, you can make it anywhere." I'll see if that statement is accurate or just lyrics to one of his favorite songs.

You're probably wondering why I'm relocating from Memphis to New York City? Before I start rambling about our unexpected and depressing move, let me introduce myself.

I am Jade Johnson, but you can call me Jade. Mom and dad call me by my entire name only when they're upset with me. I don't think it happens often, but they may tell a different story.

The name Jade was given to me by my dad, Daniel. He says a jade blesses whatever it touches and as a newborn, he thought it was fitting. Yea, I know, I know, it's kind of corny, yet cool, but that's my dad. He loves all of me, including this big hair of mine; this is probably my most distinctive feature. Although I have a very noticeable mole on my bottom right chin, my hair precedes it. I speak with a very slight lisp, but my coils scream louder. I tend to love bright colored clothing, yet my hair is what people tend to see first. It's big and tightly curled, dark as a licorice jellybean, yet soft as cotton candy. I've finally learned how to embrace it, although taming it is a challenge. I tend to wear it out in a fro or up in an oversized ponytail. Either style gives me a daily workout.

Mom had a lot of hair once, and she did the "big chop," which is basically her cutting off all processed hair. Now it's entirely natural, just like mine and she occasionally blows it out and wears it straight like it is now. Everyone back home called us twins. We share the same espresso color complexion and almond-shaped eyes. Even our names resemble each other – Jade and Jada. Coincidence, I think not.

Usually, when you see mom, you see me, unless I'm at school of course. I'm her shadow, so we're totally inseparable. She can't shake me, but the truth is, I can't shake her either. Even now, it's just mom and me on this cold airplane heading to New York City. Dad and Uncle Dave are driving the moving truck with all of our belongings, while we fly. I shouldn't complain about four hours on this plane, considering dad's route from Memphis to our new home is about sixteen hours away. My grandpa says, "sometimes when you think you have it bad; someone else may have it worse." In this case, dad has it four times worse.

Like the trip to Seattle, flying to NYC is awfully long. I used every form of entertainment I packed, and we're still in the air. I read several chapters of my book; briefly watched the in-flight movie; played a few card games with mom, and played several games on my tablet. Now I'm listening to music and choreographing a dance routine in my head. I'm trying my best to keep up with the up-tempo beat of Bruno Mars while counting down the minutes left until we land.

Before we left, my parents sat me down and discussed the reasons for moving – blah, blah, blah. I'll fill you in on all of that later. Truthfully, I have a feeling this experience is something I have to go through. I don't think any amount of pep talk could have prepared me for this new journey. So, like on a roller coaster, I buckled in. I'm not sure if I will enjoy the ride, but I hope I'm prepared for all the ups and downs, loops, turns, and possible nausea after it all.

I'm sad to leave our home in Memphis behind, but I am looking forward to seeing what New York has to offer. Although summer will be over soon, I am already excited to see how Christmas will be. I've heard from relatives and seen on TV how beautiful the holidays are. I just hope it will be the same up close! I want to visit the enormous Christmas tree at Rockefeller Center; Central Park's skating rink, and witness all the bright lights and decorations in the streets. It will be my first birthday and Christmas in the Big Apple. I wonder how big the celebration will be. I'm facing a whole lot of newness: new age; new home; new school, and both seen and unseen new experiences.

My home is, I mean, was in Memphis, Tennessee. I absolutely loved it there, but I guess it's because it's all I knew and what I was accustomed to. It's also where my grandparents and best friends are. It's where people knew me and I knew them, like a big happy family. I knew the neighborhood and I couldn't get lost and if I ever did, there were familiar faces everywhere; I always felt safe. I'm not sure if New York will be able to offer the same familiarity or even a similar security blanket. It seems like such a big city; congested and overwhelming.

One of the most crowded places in Memphis, from what dad described was Beale Street. The area was filled with tons of jazz clubs, restaurants, and many stores to shop. My parents love Jazz, but I can't say the same.

For instance, right now, I'm listening to some pop as I lay against the window seat while playing candy crush on my tablet. My hair often gets in the way, but at times like this, it serves as a nice plush pillow. For me, music has to make me want to move since I love to dance! I used to be part of my school's dance team. My crew and I love to perform. We were technicians in our craft; pretty much perfectionists! For the last two years, we were the champions in our school district competitions. Because of the move to NYC, I had to quit the dance team; I think that's one of the hardest things I had to do. I cried and cried. I felt I was letting my squad down. The sadness was deep and still is. I haven't stopped practicing. Furthermore, I consider everywhere to be my stage. It will be different looking to the left and right and not seeing Tiffany, Renee, and Josie. Josie was positioned next to Renee on my left; while Tiffany was always on my right. I miss the three of them so much! Last week I cried every day at the thought of moving away from my best friends. This is going to be such a difficult transition. I have to get used to the idea of New York being my new home and making new friends. That's what dad keeps trying to tell me, but it's easier said than done. I hope the big city is kind to this southern girl.

"Ladies and gentlemen" the pilot announces, "we're approaching LaGuardia Airport, where the local time is 4:17 p.m., with clear skies and a temperature of 93 degrees. At this time, please make sure your seat backs and tray tables are in their full upright position. Make sure your seatbelt is securely fastened..." Mom over talks the announcement with "Jade, this is it!" Her voice is full of excitement, and she reaches over to hug me. Instead, I'm pretending to sleep. I truly wish it were all a dream. I pause from playing opossum to look out the window, to be greeted with an amazing view. I can see the wings of the plane with the New York City skyline in the background as the plane prepares for landing. It's not a dream, this is my life.

Chapter 2
First Base... Not Baseball

The moment mom and I step off the aircraft, I find myself approaching first base, labeled airport terminal D. I immediately put my tablet away, it seems like I have to focus and pay close attention to where I'm walking. I feel anxious with all these people around. It feels like an episode of *The Flash*. Everyone is moving at the speed of light; even the little old man with a cane is trying to keep up before he gets trampled. Another traveler is in such a haste that she trips over her own feet, stumbles down a few steps, gets up, and quickly grabs her duffle bag as if it is a baton and continues to run her relay race through the airport.

In Memphis, we take things easy. We stroll, and don't speed walk! It seems like everyone here is in a rush or late for everything. Even the taxi line we're standing on is filled with impatient people and their heap of luggage. Fortunately, we only have two suitcases. The taxi line wraps and bends around itself like a snake. With all the haste that I'm experiencing, I'm surprised the line is moving at a slow slithering motion. There seems to be a shortage of taxis for the number of people waiting. Luckily, there are only a few passengers ahead for us to slide into second base.

In the taxi on the way to our new home in Harlem, I'm laying my head on the window, comfy in my curls, contemplating life. I've been doing this for the last few months, trying to predict how this life, home, school, friends, and many other scenarios will play out. As I daydream, I'm taking in my surroundings since it's moving in slow motion. It's almost as if the universe knew my brain needed a break from the fast-paced craziness I just witnessed at the airport. I feel like I can finally breathe and take this all in. Compared to everyone rushing earlier, the cars are now at a standstill, thanks to New York City traffic. We are in the heart of an oxymoronic rush hour. I remained quiet for most of the plane ride and now the taxi ride as well. Staring out the window, looking up at buildings that seem to reach for the clouds, I make a quick wish to disappear as their peaks did. An overpowering sadness fills my heart and suddenly my lips are moist from the tears that slip from my eyes.

I'm trying my hardest not to whimper or sniffle. I really don't want to have a discussion with mom about why I'm crying, when we both know the answer. I catch a glimpse of her from the corner of my eye and she is preoccupied on her phone and familiar sounds confirm it – tip, tap, click, tip, tip, tip tap, click, click, tip, tap, tap. The speed she types on her phone is incredible; at times you would think she is using a laptop the way her fingers move so swiftly. I'm assuming she's letting family and friends know we arrived safely or maybe she is responding to all her business messages as well. Recently, she's been busy with her online clothing boutique- where she designs and makes all the clothes herself. The business is flourishing even with us relocating here, thanks to the Internet and social media. She continues to text, all I can hear are her nails tapping on the screen composing a message. Tip, tap, click, tip, tip, tip tap, again, her quickness is insane, matching New York's vibe.

As I thought I was safe like the batter at a baseball game, her phone rings and it's a special ringtone, one that is assigned only to my dad. I already know he's going to want to speak with me, but right now, I'm too distressed to even speak with my favorite person. The best thing I can think of is to become sleeping beauty.

"Hey Jade, Jade, dad is calling. Jade?" Mom softly nudges me.

"Hey honey, how are the roads driving up?" there's a quick pause, assuming he's responding to her question. "Oh, ok. You guys are on track then huh? Meanwhile, we are stuck in so much traffic, not sure what time we should arrive at the new place. Yes, it seems like Jade is taking another one of her power naps," she continues to speak to him. As I think I'm about to strike out, I suddenly feel safe again. I sneakily open my eyes hoping the hair in my face is enough to camouflage them. Instead, I make eye contact with the taxi driver by accident. His eyes grin at me. He's been watching the entire time, can you believe it? I hope he doesn't tell; I hope he's on my team or at least just a spectator.

After what feels like another flight on wheels, the taxi finally comes to a halt in front of a very tall building. It's not as tall as the skyscrapers I saw during the ride here, but still very tall. My eyes quickly scan what I can see from the car windows. It's definitely not the south; this two-block radius has other apartment buildings in the area, grocery stores, a restaurant, and other random businesses. I see delivery men on bicycles; people walking; a fabulously dressed group of woman strutting and talking; an attractive couple holding hands; a father pushing a stroller; a mother wiping the tears of her daughter because she fell off her scooter. Good to know I'm not the only one that is an emotional wreck today.

I feel like a fish in a bowl, just observing it all. An old man walking his dog, but it looks more like the dog is walking him.

The area is filled with parked cars and vehicles driving up and down the streets as they play their music at whatever volume they choose and honk their horns as if they are part of a band creating the soundtrack for my new life entitled "Madness." To add to the noise, I hear, "Jade, we're here!" Mom says ecstatically as her voice pierces my eardrums. Even the driver looks startled. I crush her excitement by rolling my eyes. As my eyes begin to roll, I try to stop because I know the repercussions that will follow, and they won't be pretty. Before I could open my mouth to apologize, I'm already being yelled at.

"Jade Johnson! I will make those eyes get stuck in the back of your head!" Mom says with confusion. Although I am wrong, I still can't find the words to apologize. "What's your issue?" she questions.

My issue? I can think of a few. The streets are full of people... people aren't wearing smiles... my friends are not here... I don't have my grandparents close any more... nothing looks the same... everything is different... why must I listen to this man playing his music as he walks pass the taxi? I still don't understand why we left our big house to live in a building with other people and we don't even have a backyard. Sadness is overtaking me. I just want to cry. I decide I am not going to leave the cab; the driver is going to take me back to the airport. I refuse to get out of this yellow car. No way am I going to live in New York. I want no piece of this big apple. Everyone keeps saying this city is big, but with all these people and all these cars, it seems overcrowded. Since it's so big, it won't miss me. That's the rant in my head. Instead, I edit my monologue, my tone, and facial expression to say, "I miss Memphis" I begin to tear up.

"Sweetie, please, we went through this already. We are relocating because of dad's job promotion with his accounting firm and my clothing line. There are a lot more opportunities for us here. We both explained this to you. I know it is going to be

9

hard to adjust but change is good sometimes, and dad is so happy about this change. I'm super excited, and we both want you to be happy as well." Mom says in her sweetest voice trying to console, but I can't and don't want to comprehend it.

"Well, I don't think this change is good. Grandpa always says if it's not broken then don't fix it. Memphis isn't broken. There was nothing wrong with our home! But there is everything wrong with moving here . . . and I don't know anyone; anyone at all, mom." As my voice cracks, tears roll down my face. I wipe my eyes, I see the taxi driver witnessing our entire conversation again through that same rear view mirror. This time his eyes are playing ping-pong searching for emotions from mom and me. I promise, I try to hold these tears back, but reality sets in. I'm actually here in a foreign city and the only people I know are my parents. Memphis is all I know and I'm going through shock right now.

"Sweetie, I don't know anyone either. All we have is each other and that's enough. Eventually, we will make new friends and acquaintances. Until then, we have to give this city a chance. Let's finish this conversation upstairs because the cab driver has other people to pick up and drop off," she says with her biggest smile as she tries to comfort me.

"I know, he's dropping me off at the airport," I reply sternly as I fold my arms to imply my seriousness. Mom is trying to be very patient. I can tell by the way she bites down on the right side of her bottom lip and inhales deeply, and as she exhales, air escapes her lips. Again, I roll my eyes. This time she threatens to have them permanently removed. I have no idea what is overtaking me, that's making me give her such gestures. I never talk back to her. I need to compose myself. Maybe if I close my eyes, it will all be a nightmare. I did just that, only to reopen them and notice my scenery is the same. What is supposed to feel like a blink back to reality, is not working; mom thinks I'm giving her more attitude. Her face looks even more discombobulated. Her eyebrows furrow in the center of her forehead. Now her lips are pursed like a duck's beak. She slowly eases her sunglasses from her face to launch a strike from her lightning eyes.

Chapter 3
Home

I quickly peel myself off the seats of the cab to get out. The driver is foreign. I wonder if he misses his homeland as well. "Thank you, sir." I force a smile to my secret teammate and close the taxi door. I stretch, I yawn, and I take a good look at the building that is now called "home." I quickly analyze the premises, this time I'm standing on the sidewalk, which gives me a very different perspective; however, it's just not what I am accustomed to. Plus, I am emotionally distressed, especially with dad not being here. I can be such a drama queen and a whiner at times. Usually, the only thing that can soothe me is him. It's something about his deep raspy voice when he calls me his "Precious Gem." It's very comforting. I know, I know, stop judging me, but I'm such a daddy's girl.

Speaking of my savior; dad and Uncle Dave, also called Uncle D, is scheduled to arrive tomorrow with the rest of our belongings. Believe it or not, he left with the moving truck a few hours before we left Memphis airport and I overheard him telling mom the drive to New York will be about 16 to 20 hours depending on traffic. That's practically an entire day of driving, insane if you ask me. If he is stuck in traffic like what we were in earlier, it will be even longer, I assume. That's my dad; he will do what he has to do for his family without complaining. He says often "Complaining only slows down the process of completing a task." I need to take that advice right now.

Wow! Wow! Wow! I slide into third base and enter a luxurious lobby, where a doorman greets us. "Mom, this is kind of fancy huh!" She looks at me over her sunglasses and simply smiles and then finally releases the tension from moments ago in the taxi.

As she speaks with the doorman at the front desk, her shades are now in her hands, as her fingers gesture for me to stay close. I find myself cheering up slowly; I think it's due to the bright yellow painted walls in the lobby. The ceiling lamps resemble a chandelier, not overly extravagant, but still very pretty and bright. The yellow walls with the light cascading on it, along with other pieces of furniture, offer a welcoming feeling, although not kid friendly. I'm trying my very best to stand still and not explore the lobby by touching things and picking them up. The ambiance of the lobby is absolutely beautiful and it's miraculously changing my mood by filling me up with positive energy. This reminds me of when my art teacher, Mr. Bowers, explained how certain colors affect people's emotions. Imagine what a black wall would have done to my mood when I entered the building with my current state of mind.

We then arrive at the twelfth floor and prepare to slide into home. We are introduced to another paint color, a light green one, similar to the inside of a kiwi fruit. I think this color may help mom's mood… Her eyebrows are no longer crunched together, and her mood is no longer stale and hard as weeks old bread. I am trying to break the ice and lighten the mood and match her energy and enthusiasm from earlier. "This is it!" I said trying with a big but false smile as mom attempts to open the door. The door swings open and unfolds our new home; I am surprised by what is revealed. I am in shock to see how nice and big it is! Finally, a genuine smile cracks through mom's face. She is just as pleased as I am and it's a relief to see her mood shift gears.

Dad loves colored walls as well. Back in Memphis, every room had a different feel to it. I'm pretty sure this home will not be any different. Our kitchen is smaller compared to what dad is used to cooking in; I see we are all making compromises. Although our furniture and belongings are not inside, it's still a nice spacious layout. Right now, I see it all as a massive dance studio, and with that thought, I drop my favorite bookbag by the door, press play to "beat it," a Michael Jackson song in my head and perform an old dance routine from my dance team. A few spins, side slides, the kick and finished off with his famous toe stand. Mom watches, as I own the stage. I take a bow and receive imaginary flowers; air kisses are blown into an audience of white walls, and I exit stage left and run off to find my dressing room.

Found it! It's decent; it's big enough for all my things and a large wall mirror. Who doesn't like to pose, dance, and model in front of the mirror? Well, at least I do. All this space makes me very happy. I need to call a truce and cease-fire to her occasionally disappointed stares. Time to go make peace and wave my white flag.

Knock knock...

"Come on in sweetie," mom says behind her half-opened bedroom door. As I enter, I notice she is already unpacking things from her carryon. Of course, she is. She's such a neat freak.

"Mom, I'm soooo sorry." I extend my arms to give her a big hug.

"You better be, your dad and I went through a lot to buy this condo." She kisses my forehead and hugs me back a little tighter. As she releases from the hug, her earring gets caught in my hair.

This tends to happen often, but this time it's a quicker escape.

"Wait, we're not renting?" I'm curious as I follow her around our new home.

"We bought this condominium. You can call it a condo for short," she says as we walk into the kitchen.

"Is that the same as an apartment?" Still inquiring, I ask.

"This building has both condos and apartments for rent. The apartments are rented and the condos are owned. Like when we go to the skating rink, we can rent the skates for $5 or we can come with our own. At the end of the day, if you rented the skates, you have to give them back because they are not yours. However, in this case, we own this unit, so when we move we will have the opportunity to sell it. Do you understand?" she says, waiting to load on more information; she continues to open each cabinet to do a quick inspection.

"Yeah!" I skip away and start to dance midway towards my room. I needed a brief bolt because she would have gone on forever trying to explain. She will say the same thing in 10 different ways. Usually, when I don't understand, I will say I do. But I will wait until she is not around, and ask dad to explain it. He has a special way of simplifying things.

From my room, I slide into the empty living room ready to perform my dance routine, "1, 2, 1, 2, and 3" as I count out the steps to continue, I am interrupted... mom yells from the kitchen, "Are you ready to start cleaning?" I guess she saw something suspicious in those cabinets.

Confusion masks my face. Wait, clean! Isn't this a new home? Why are we cleaning? It looks spotless? Rather than ask, I simply yell back, "Sure!" I quickly did my finale with another one-two-step, followed by a spin. Then I slide my way back to where she is. Before we start, I need to figure out what we're going to eat. That way I have something to look forward to after this pseudo cleanup.

I prompt mom that dinnertime is approaching, which means

take-out since we do not have any pots, pans, plates, or utensils yet. "Yes, food! I am thinking the same thing. What would you like?" She asks. "Ummm, teriyaki chicken and lo-mein?" My taste buds are craving something sweet and tangy. Ohhhh, I just realize this is my first official meal in this city. Let's hope they don't disappoint the two of us, meaning my belly and me.

"Ok, let's see what's in this area." After searching for places to order, I hear her on the phone asking twenty-one questions. Mom tends to ask a lot of questions, as do I. Maybe that's where I get it from. After her interrogation, I hear her placing the order.

"Small chicken teriyaki with lo mein, and please add extra meat. Yes, the additional charge is quite alright. Yes, and also 3 rolls. Ummm, I will have the spider, dragon, aaaannnnnd, ummm a Philadelphia roll?" A brief moment of silence takes over allowing mom to catch her breath and gather her thoughts. "How much is that? How long will it take?" Another brief pause follows by "Thank you so much." She disconnects from the call.

Hearing her order our meals, I become concerned and my mind fills with disbelief when I hear her say dragon, spider, and Philadelphia. I wait for her to get off the phone to speak. "Dragons and spiders?"

"Girl, you're so silly. I ordered your food and a few specialty rolls from this Asian restaurant, which has great reviews online." She completely misconstrued my seriousness as silliness.

"Mom, for real. Did the dragon and spider go to Philadelphia?" I said as a joke, but am still stumped by what she ordered.

"I tell you, you truly get your sense of humor from your dad, you silly girl."

"For real, I'm serious?" I need her to understand at this point an explanation is needed.

"Alright, alright silly girl. I ordered sushi. Dragon rolls have a mixture of crab, cucumber, eel, and avocado. While the spider rolls have soft-shell-crab and avocado. And the Philadelphia is a combination of salmon and cream cheese," she says, sounding quite winded, but still ready to explain further. I figure, let me interrupt, to give her a second to catch her breath and for me to get more clarity.

"You mean cream cheese that we put on a bagel; cream cheese that you make cheesecake with; cream cheese with fish? I'm not sure about that mom, and you ordered a spider? Why would you want to eat anything that is called a spider?" I said with my most inquisitive voice.

"Well, they all taste soooo yummy," mom says with excitement.

When it comes to food, I will try many things as long as there is some type of meat or protein in it. My dad jokes around that I am a meat-a-tarian, which is not a real word, but that's his corny way of saying that I eat a lot of meat. Mom and dad try to trick me by loading my plate up with veggies and then they pour on meat-flavored gravy, hoping to make me enjoy them more. It works! I think with each meal, they put less and less gravy on, but more and more veggies. I got my eyes on them, they are not tricking me.

As of late, mom's meals look like rabbit food, mainly vegetables, and very small servings of meat. During some meals, she won't have any meat at all. That's why I'm surprised she ordered sushi. My dad, on the other hand, is a vegetarian; and I think, he is secretly trying to convert mom and me, one at a time. I think his sermons on eating solely vegetables have seeped through to mom. Years ago, she always had an eclectic palette and would try almost anything. Now, she prefers a vegetable-based diet; as for me, not so much. I love my protein, hence, the nicknames meatatarian or carnivore.

I tasted sushi once and was not a fan. I'm now open to giving it a second chance. Hey, maybe New York can create a new me. Ha, saying it didn't even sound believable. I'm thinking about asking her to call back and order me a specialty roll, but it may be best to just try hers. I don't want to waste food and have her give me that look. For my mom, that look involves her eyebrows wrinkled and meeting in the middle of her forehead. You guys know the look I'm talking about, that look our parents give us when they are about to lecture us on something or simply say, "I told you so." Right now, her face is beyond pleasant and we are in a happy place.

"Food is ordered, and delivery is expected in about an hour which is great because we can get the cleaning done in the meantime. I want us to wipe down the shelves, windows, and all mirrors, counters, and mop these floors before dad comes with our things tomorrow." She runs through her mental task list.

I can't resist, I have to ask, "Mom, why are we cleaning again?"

"We are not sure how the previous owners kept their home. I can assume that management cleaned this unit. The best way to make sure is what?" as she queued me to finish her statement.

"To do it yourself," I said, feeling like I was in a classroom. As I mentioned earlier, mom is kind of a clean freak. Time to clean, a clean house I guess.

Although the house looks spotless, we are cleaning as if it isn't. With every wipe and every sweep, I have a perplex look on my face and I sporadically look over at mom to see if her face matches mine. Instead, she's singing and humming to the songs that are playing on the radio. There is very little to no dirt residue showing up on the paper towels we're using to wipe. And when I sweep, nothing gathers on the floor. As a child, I've learned we have to do as we are told, although the thinking of our parents and adults will not always make sense to us. They say one day it will.

Since it isn't strenuous work, we finish rather quickly. Within minutes, our doorbell rings. It has to be the food because, ahhhhh, we don't know anyone here. It's the delivery guy; mom pays for the food and tips him. I notice, wherever we go, both my parents usually tip people, like the delivery guy, grocery bagger, salon technician when mom gets her manicures, pedicures, and facials, and anyone else that does great service. Of all the questions I've asked, I never thought to question them why they tip so frequently?

As I'm about to inquire, the pleasant aroma of the food tickles my nose. Suddenly, I am hungrier than I realize. I am actually excited to taste mom's dragon and spider rolls. The presentation of it is nicely done. It really emulates a creepy crawler; it looks more like art you admire than food you would eat. The smell reminds me it needs to be devoured. However, what I really want to taste is the Philadelphia, which looks very simplistic. It's mom's favorite and I need to know why. I still can't imagine how raw fish and cream cheese taste. I am open to trying it and beyond curious.

We have a blanket already laid out on the floor. We place the food in the middle and I attempt to eat with chopsticks. Mom can do it really well, but I have a bit of difficulty. I can't figure out how to hold the two sticks in one hand. Mom attempts to give me a tutorial, but with each attempt, the sticks fall. We both look at each other intensely yet trying not to laugh and agree with our eyes that we should just eat. She holds a piece of the dragon roll in her chopsticks and put it in my mouth. I bite it cautiously, chew slowly, but once it hits my tongue the flavors are absolutely delicious. At this point, I no longer want what I ordered.

I swallow the first bite and immediately open my mouth for more. It is amazing; I beckon her to let me try the others.

"See, this is why I tell you, you need to give different cultures a try because you may find something in it you like and actually enjoy." She's about to start preaching, and like I told you before, she can go on and on and on like a radio with no off switch. "I know you're right. You are so right, that I think to teach me a lesson, we should switch foods!" We both laugh hard and she still says "No" with a smile.

"Don't you think I need to embrace and appreciate the culture by eating their food?" I ask trying to be cunning.

"Sweetie you are embracing their culture by eating your own food. How's the teriyaki by the way? The lo-mein looks delicious." We laugh again. She gives in and gives me another piece of each roll. Thank you, New York, so far so good; first the building, then our actual home, and now sushi. Keep impressing me please, pretty please.

After we ate, we play a few games of Uno. I keep winning of course; I'm great with piling up my pairs. Skip – skip still my turn. Reverse – Reverse still my turn. Ohhh, don't forget to draw 2, and another 2 and another 2. Mom tries to add her draw 2, but of course, I have one that I saved just in case. Better now than never; draw 10. She's now ready to say game over at this point. She reluctantly keeps playing, I think in hopes of at least winning one game. However, after I win three games with no losses, suddenly she's exhausted. We both decide to get some rest.

An air mattress is our bed for the night and she is my security blanket. The next morning we are awoken by dad opening the door. It's such a familiar way to start the day in an unfamiliar place.

Chapter 4
Box by Box by Box

"Good morning sleeping beauties," dad says as he kisses my forehead and then gives mom a kiss on her lips that create a muuuuuaaah sound effect.

"I have breakfast!" he says as I reach over for a hug. I am so delighted to see him; I glance over at mom; she is too. When the two of them are together, you can tell how much they really love each other. At least I can tell by the way they stare at each other when the other is not looking. Even the way dad prepares the fast food breakfast he brought us. It's presented with such love and care as if he cooked it himself.

We sit and eat, and discuss yesterday. I explain my anxiousness on the plane and how everyone was bumping into us at the airport because they were all rushing. I gloss over my attempt to hold the taxi driver hostage and our efforts to clean a house that seems to be already clean. I also share how I tried sushi again and enjoyed it this time around. His eyes show varied emotions from sympathy to confusion, to still puzzled, to indifference, to being pleased overall. It is such an exhausting, yet entertaining day.

Shortly after my report, dad proceeds to fill us in on how long their drive was.

"That's the longest drive I have ever done." He says, exhaling slowly and shaking his head.

"Did you stop at rest stops to sleep at least?" I ask because he looks exhausted. The bags under his eyes are beyond full and heavier than anything he lifted the day prior.

"We did, but not for long, stopping only makes the journey that much longer" just then, the doorbell rings. Dad opens the door and it is Uncle Dave. As I run to hug him, I put on my brakes before I crash into him and the beverages he is carrying. Whew! That was a close call considering mom and I just swept and mopped our immaculate floors.

Uncle Dave and dad are complete opposites, although they ironically call each other twin. They are not actual twins, but "Irish Twins," which means they are eleven months apart; dad is the oldest. Dad towers many people in height, and he is very slim, similar to myself. When he was a child, he would get teased for his height and was called the nickname spaghetti. The mean kids' rationale for the name was because he was so tall and lanky and his skin complexion wasn't too far from the shade of uncooked spaghetti. Meanwhile, Uncle D is short and his entire body is covered in muscles, but as a kid, he was very heavy. Now, if you stare at him long enough, you can even see muscles in his face. He seems like a statue that's chiseled to resemble the Greek gods; although he has a deep dark chocolate complexion. I find it interesting how he and dad are almost the complete opposite in physical attributes. Dad explains that it is all based on genetics.

My grandma, from dad's side, has very fair skin; often she is mistaken for a white lady. My grandpa has dark skin like Uncle D. He explains that genetics is the reason why he and his brother have different skin tones. Uncle D does not have freckles, but dad does, like a banana with all the spots on it when it's becoming over ripened. That was one of the comments that mean kids would tease him with as well. Although he was badgered as a child with names like spaghetti and banana face, I still cannot relate entirely because I have never been teased. Most people often stare at my hair, or at the enlarged mole on my chin. They only stare; I haven't experienced any mean words with it.

After eating, dad and Uncle D start bringing up the furniture and all the boxes out of the moving truck. Instantly, our new empty home is an absolute mess and full of clutter like a toy chest filled to the top with absolutely no room for anything else. Dad and Uncle D are now sweaty with multiple sweat beads on their faces; the beads are dripping down their necks and temporarily staining their shirts that now have a slightly pungent smell attached to it. After all, they are putting in hard labor.

There are boxes everywhere. Of course, there's some type of organization where each box lands. Mom turns into a moving-box-traffic-cop making sure there are no incidents and that our nice floors don't get scratched. As she gives directions, I give out cold glasses of water when needed.

"Put that in the kitchen."

"That goes in our bedroom."

"Put it here."

"Place it there."

"Hey, hey, please watch my floors."

"Put it there for now."

"Jade take this bag to your room."

"Ummm, you can place the couch over there for now."

"That belongs in the bathroom."

"Please be careful with that."

This goes on for a while. Both my dad and Uncle D are moving like perfectly orchestrated robots with one mission- empty the truck and to do what mom says. They seem very dehydrated and the blazing temperature of 98 degrees outside is not helping. I assume that since New York is up north, it shouldn't be so sweltering, but I am so wrong. With each glass of ice-cold water, their thirst seems to get quenched slightly. Eventually, the truck becomes empty, and in exchange, our home is filled with boxes; there are boxes and more boxes. What seems like chaos to me is perfect organization to mom. Boxes are everywhere but they are labeled by room and purpose. Letting us know what is inside each of them and where they belong. Of course, mom delegates that.

The guys go back to drop off the moving truck, and mom and I begin to unpack the kitchen. The drinking glasses and plates are protected in bubble wrap. I can't help but pop them a few times. These little things are so addictive. It's like once you pop one, you can't help but to pop more and more and more and more until it's snatched out of your hands.

"Jade please stop and continue to empty out these boxes," she pleads as she accidentally pops it too and we both chuckle.

"Sure, how long do you think it will take to get the house in order?" I question because I already know she calculated the time and I can tell all this clutter is making her anxious. I can tell in general this move makes her a little uptight; she is usually more relaxed and at times playful; and it usually takes a lot for me to ruffle her feathers and annoy her. In all fairness, I have also been a little bratty. Ok, very bratty.

"We really should be finished by tonight." She replies with confidence; I almost dropped the glass I'm unwrapping. Thank God for good reflexes.

"Tonight? Mom, do you see how many boxes and bags there

are?" I questioned again. I'm very good at math, but quite frankly this is not adding up.

She simply looks around and takes a deep breath, and continues to fill our empty kitchen cabinets. A sigh softly exits my lips, but no words follow. I continue to unpack.

Mom and I unpack box after box, after box with old school dance music playing in the background. Mom is in some type of trance as she is unpacking and singing along to every song. I've never seen her like this. As she is performing, her microphone interchanges from a spatula from the kitchen, to a stirring spoon. The kitchen counter is her drum. The jars of spices and seasoning are her tambourines.

She swings her hips from side to side, synchronizing to the beat. Her fingers slow down the tempo as her imaginary piano suspends in the air. She is truly a one-woman-imaginary-band and I am definitely entertained. I enjoy every minute that the beats and rhythms play. I knew very little words until a Whitney Houston or Michael Jackson song played. At that point, I join mom on stage to have a mini-concert starring us, The Johnsons. We enjoy an inter-mission when dad and Uncle D return.

They pick up where they left off... moving, pushing, and lifting all things heavy. Within a few hours, the kitchen is complete and the living room is in order. The only rooms left to organize and unpack are the bedrooms.

I am not looking forward to doing anything else. I'm so sleepy and hungry again. As these thoughts begin to take me hostage, dad comes to my rescue.

"Alright, alright... that's enough. Let's put a pause on this, freshen up and let's go out to dinner."

I can tell that mom would rather keep organizing and sorting our home, but instead, she stuffs the used bubble wrap in the trash and walks away from box number 17 and simply says, "OK honey, we can finish this up tomorrow."

Tomorrow is here, and my room is still a mess. I did not unpack one box yet. Mom already suggested before we left for dinner that I should have everything unpacked by the end of the week. Look at all these boxes. I wonder how long it will take me to unpack. As soon as I said that, I hear a knock on my bedroom door. "Knock, knock, can I come in?" Dad says with a smile in his voice.

"Yes, come on in," I said with a yawn and stretch, moving all this hair from my face.

"Well, good morning! Are you hungry?" he says in his raspy voice.

"Morning dad. I'm not hungry; I'm actually still full from dinner last night. The food was sooo delicious and filling. I'll get to these boxes in a few."

"Jade, by Friday, I want everything in order. That is more than enough time. Do you see how many boxes your mom and I have to unpack?"

"I do, but there are two of you unpacking versus just me. Plus I helped with all the kitchen boxes. Dad, I really don't think two days is realistic," I said searching for a compromise.

Dad stood emotionless and said "Of course it is realistic, but let's not make this another one of your adventures. Although I can't see how you can, somehow I know you will."

"Oh Dad, anything and everything can be an adventure," I say with a huge grin of confidence.

"Jade, Friday everything must be unpacked," he says sternly.

"Yes Dad, but is Friday mom's deadline too?" Dad gives me one of those don't-play-with-me-looks and walks out of my room, leaving the door cracked open for the steam he blew off to escape.

Hmmmmm, as I stand in the center of all the boxes, I can't help but to scratch my head and ponder on why Friday? Are we having company over? Regardless of the reason, let me start unpacking. As I said before, often we have to do what we are told and figure out why later.

How should I do this, what will make it more fun? I know! I will unpack everything first and put things away as I pick them up. Yes, that's what I'll do.

Boxes are emptied one by one. At first, I start to make a neat pile, but with all the boxes that are in my room, the pile gets out of control. Next thing I know, there are multiple piles of clothes everywhere, books scattered, random toys peeking out of the clothes – it is so untidy and so much clutter in my room that I have to bring the boxes out into the hallway. This will also give my parents the illusion that I am fulfilling their request.

Now, I'm exhausted. I look around the room to witness the beautiful madness I created. In doing so, I glance at a pile that's mostly clothes and it looks so soft and comfortable. I think I'll take a nap; I know I shouldn't stop, but all this unpacking makes me really tired. Glancing at the time on my tablet, I notice only an hour went by, although it felt so much longer. I shrug and convince myself that a nap would recharge me enough to finish later.

Suddenly, I am at this ice cream shop back home in Memphis and Mr. Walker is preparing me my favorite ice cream cone: Mmmmm, three scoops of pineapple and coconut. I know it's not the popular flavors of vanilla or chocolate, but it's so delicious. You must give it a try. It is a hot summer day and the ice cream is melting from the boiling southern sun. The cream is dripping down the cone and on to my hands. It becomes a race against time to finish it before the sun does. As I am about to devour my melted treat, I'm startled by "Jadeeeeeeeeeeeeeee Johnson!" I drop my ice cream cone, it splatters on the ground and then on my sneakers. I am so upset because I could not even taste how yummy it really was. I woke up so confused.

After realizing I just hit reality, I stare at dad as he stands in front of me holding a bowl of fruit, and sounding as if he is speaking another language. Everything sounds like gibberish. Since I am still in a slumber, he decides to translate.

"Why would you unpack like this?" he says in frustration.

"Oh Dad, I have this under control. It will all get put away by Friday. I promise!" I continue to plead my case, "You didn't say how to get it done, as long as it's done by Friday, right dad?" I decide to hush my mouth; after all, I was supposed to get grounded before we moved here. It's a long story, but I promise to tell you all about it soon.

Dad is baffled by the mess and my nonchalant tone; he walks out of my room without saying anything else. This time he allows the door to slam on its own and he takes the bowl back with him. Am I wrong? He said to have it done by Friday. Not once did he say how to do it. He should have been more specific. I don't understand why he is so upset. More importantly, I don't understand why he didn't give me the bowl of fruit that I know was meant for me. It looked so refreshing. Like I told him, everything should be an adventure and having fun through it all is what truly makes it memorable. I guess I should start getting this room in order again.

Chapter 5
Pile by Pile

Shirts get hung in the closet; PJs get folded and placed in a draw; shoes on the rack; dolls in the toy-chest; books on the shelf, ooh, and my diary gets hidden under my mattress. Do you have one too? Where do you hide yours? Shorts and skirts are folded, and socks are rolled as I continue to sort out my room.

Slowly, everything begins to go into its correct home. All of this left me exhausted and finally hungry. Looking at a pile next to my bookshelf, and another by the door, and finally the one I'm lying on, makes me realize I still have much more to organize. Ugh, I wish I had a little sister that could help me. As I am unpacking, I see so many things that I absolutely love and things that I do not enjoy anymore or simply do not hold my attention, like my dolls. I keep them because they were gifts, but I feel like I truly outgrew them. This includes my Winnie the Pooh teddy bear; I reach for it. I hug it tightly, recalling my emotions, the first day it was given to me by my Aunt Kimmy. At this moment, I realize that I am not ready to separate from my Pooh Bear. Nope, he shall go where he always sits, right on my bookshelf.

I make room at his usual hangout spot, on the third shelf, at the right side corner. Pooh also serves as a bookend to keep the books standing in that row. I place him in his snugged spot, and it dawns on me that I really have a lot of books. I love to read so much, that within the last year, dad had to replace my old bookcase and buy me something larger to accommodate all my books, and have room for new ones as well.

The six feet tall, eight shelves, espresso brown bookcase is already almost filled. The top two shelves include an encyclopedia collection that used to belong to mom. I still don't understand why she donated them to me. I remember saying to her "That's what Google is for." She insisted, and they are now part of my reading collection. Besides Britannica A-Z, all the books that are currently in the bookcase, I have already read. Looking at it now, I am amazed that I have read that many books.

If I could guess, I probably have over 200 books. My collection includes: The People Could Fly; Charlotte's Web; Huckleberry Finn; Oliver Twist; The Snowy Day; Pippi Longstocking; Nappy Hair; Nancy Drew; Diary of Anne Frank, and a few others that I absolutely love. Dad calls them classics because they have been around a very long time, some before I was even born and some before he was born. One day, I will attempt to count them again. If I had a little sister, I could order her to do so. Being an only child can feel lonely at times, but it also has its advantages as well. Right now it sucks, I could really use some help organizing this room.

I am tired of cleaning up. Let's peek and see what's happening outside of my room, hopefully, all the smoke has cleared. Although there isn't any smoke, I can smell an amazing aroma coming from the kitchen. Many times, the smell is so deliciously strong that it stops me in my tracks. This time, I hesitate because dad is already disappointed with me. With mom out running errands, and not being present for the episode earlier, the exchange in my bedroom was not as challenging. I'm sure dad will discuss with her what took place. They seem to talk about everything.

"Hey," I bellow out to fill the silent air and shyly creep into the living room area, which is adjacent to the kitchen.

"Yes, Jade," he says dryly as he stirs the mysterious contents in the pot.

"Oh nothing, I respond, just a little bit hungry. What are you cooking?"

"Hungry from cleaning up that room of yours, I hope?" he asks.

"Hungry for your food," I said trying to be playful.

"Is something wrong?" He inquires.

"Oh nothing, I'm just a little bit hungry. What are you cooking?" I ask a second time.

"Hungry from cleaning up that room of yours, I hope." He supposes.

"Hungry for your food," patronizing him as I slowly creep towards the kitchen with a smile.

"Hungry from cleaning up that room of yours, I hope." He repeats.

"Hungry for what's in that pot." I'm creeping closer towards it, with a twinkle in my eye.

"Hungry from cleaning up that room of yours, I hope," his fourth time repeating himself, but this time, he is in no way trying to repeat himself, he's not an actor trying to memorize a script for a speech or a play. Dad usually does not repeat himself at all. I really am pushing my luck. Let's go a little further.

As I tip-toe to see what's on the menu, he insists, "Hungry for what —" Before I could even finish my rehearsed statement, he sternly cuts me off. "Jade Johnson, are you close to cleaning up your room?" There goes his tone again.

"Oh dad, I started. I am just taking a break; a food break. I exhausted myself by cleaning. Now it's time to refuel." I express.

"Good! In that case, I'm making spaghetti and homemade meatballs." Dad announces.

"Sounds great and smells delicious. Can you make it cheesy?" I request.

"Sure, check the fridge, there should be some cheese on the middle shelf to the left, next to the milk," he directs me.

My eyes scan the insides of the fridge, using his cues to quickly reach for it as I simultaneously ask myself: when did my parents go food shopping?

"Can I help?" I ask as I begin to open up the package.

"Sure, I thought you just came for a tasting as usual. As much as you eat, I still have no idea where the weight goes," He says jokingly appointing me as his sous-chef.

"Oh dad, it all goes to one place," I inform him.

"And where is that?" he asks curiously.

"My head, of course, that's why I am so smart," I say with a giggle.

He steps back laughing, allowing me to add the cheese. Laughing with me, instead of at me, I hope. I add enough cheese and stir it into the sauce. Since dad is a vegetarian, he has a separate pot of marinara sauce cooking without any meat.

Once everything is complete in the kitchen, the two of us gather at the table that didn't exist 24 hours earlier. Dad makes me a nice big plate of cheesy spaghetti and meatballs with sautéed spinach on the side. Whenever he cooks, he always makes a side of vegetables. I choose not to even complain, I just eat them. However, a few years ago, I was very resistant.

With dad being a vegetarian, I never understood how could he cook something so well that he does not eat. How can he make something like a meatball taste so divine and he doesn't taste it to know that it's seasoned beyond perfection? He says he tastes the food with his nose. Have you seen my dad's nose? It's pretty large, and mom loves every inch of it. My belly seems to be made for his cooking, and I thank God for it.

When he makes meatballs, he makes them really big, like the size of a lemon. He places three of them surrounded by noodles that are al-dente and buried with his homemade marinara sauce. You can see the steam escaping from the plate, almost as if it's a caution sign blinking to warn me to slow down. I take one more smell of the amazing ingredients combined. I quickly begin to stuff so much of the food in my mouth and instantly my tongue gets burned by the obvious hot food.

I make a ridiculous sound to try to cool off my burning tongue, but never release the hot food out of my mouth. Why do we do that sometimes? Wouldn't it be less painful to just spit it out? Nope, within a few minutes, the food is gone and my plate is clean, almost as if the furious tornado JJ came and left very little evidence that any food was ever present. The only remnants are streaks of marinara sauce.

"Jade, did you just inhale that food?" Dad questions out of confusion, as if he does not know how fast I eat.

"I sure did, and it was delicious." I give him a big kiss and decide to watch some TV; he shakes his head in disbelief.

"Did you even chew? Did you at least say your grace?" Dad interrogates me.

"Yes and yes," I reply happily and satisfied.

I place my clean, yet dirty plate in the sink, and slowly walk to the couch. Dad is already watching the sports channel. I feel like a bear planning its hibernation. I fix my eyes on the television screen and watch highlights of a basketball game. It seems like my eyes are watching it, but I slowly drift off as I lay comfortably on the couch with my feet propped up on dad's lap.

"Jade. Jade, are you sleeping?" A voice softly asks, taking me out of my slumber. Duh, I'm sleeping; my eyes are closed and my breathing is heavy. My out-loud response is "Huh? Oh, hey mom. When did you come in?" I yawn and stretch out the remaining tiredness in me.

"Did you eat?" She asks, although she already probably knows the answer.

"Yes, and it was so good; dad left your plate in the microwave."

My eyes search the living room and kitchen for him.

"Speaking of, where is your father?" I shrug my shoulders. "I'm not sure, he was just here." I look around for him as well. He must have moved gently, yet swiftly, to not interrupt my nap. Although what felt like a few minutes was actually about an hour nap. I then seized that moment to change the channel that's still on sports center.

"What did you get yourself into today?" Mom asks as if she has been prepped.

"I was exercising."

"Exercising?" She's baffled.

"Oh yeah, I had a real workout," I continue to set the trap.

"Oh really, what exercises were you doing?" Mom cross-examines.

"Folding and hanging up clothes, unpacking boxes and filling up my bookcase," I said proudly.

"Really? That must have been a real workout," mom says as she walks away to look for her husband, and while carrying a shopping bag of a shimmery blue fabric peeking out.

He couldn't have gone far. It's not like we are in our old house where we had so many different rooms. Here, we only have three bedrooms. She could just scream his name and he will hear her. If we were in Memphis, I would have to run upstairs, downstairs, sometimes to the basement to find him, and other times outside in the backyard or on the porch. I used to tell him he should keep a walkie-talkie on him at all times, so if I need him I could radio him "10-4 do you copy?" "Roger that," he could reply. She found him in the office, also known as, the storage room. Don't tell mom I call it that.

Inside the storage room, dad has many rolled up drawings; tape measures; a very large ruler; drills, and multiple toolboxes, as if one is not enough. There is a lonesome box of papers stacked up in no special order. He's a man of many trades. His nine to five is being an accountant, but he is also a freelance contractor, and of course, my chef. He is not the most organized person; he expresses the opposite of mom's clean freak tendencies. Looking at this room, one would question which earthquake came and left it in such disarray?

Our condo is quite different from where we came from. In Memphis, we lived in a pretty big house as I mentioned before. Our entire community was residential. The streets in my neighborhood were not crammed with cars, because many of the vehicles get parked in a garage or driveway. I was able to ride my bike up and down the streets freely without hearing a horn honking at me, or a car trying to avoid hitting people on the sidewalks.

Living in New York, we are now living in a building. There are nineteen floors and each floor has eight units. The top floor has a unit called a penthouse, which means it is huge and probably much nicer according to mom. The entire building has one hundred-nine units. Oh yeah, math is my favorite subject. I guess I get the numbers thing from dad, he is great with numbers, which is one of the reasons he's an accountant. He deals with numbers every day at work. We both love math. I can add, multiply, and divide very well and quickly. Usually, I don't need a pencil and paper or a calculator. I do it all in my head. I'm not quite sure how I do it, but somehow my brain just understands and calculates the answer. Mom said, "It's a gift."

I wish both my parents realized that living in Memphis was a gift, that way we wouldn't have to leave. I tried using that line on them before we moved to New York, but obviously, it didn't work. I said, mom always says we must appreciate a gift. Dad looks at me, patiently waiting for me to get to my point. I added "Well, isn't this house a gift from God? Isn't it something we must appreciate like any other gift?" I listened closely for him to agree.

"Well sweetie, yes it's a gift. Mom's talent and skill as a fashion designer are truly a gift from God as well. And even though we appreciate this home, we also must nurture mom's talent. Do you understand the difference?" I nodded. "With that said, we are moving to New York to help launch your mother's career," he kindly rebutted. "God also blessed me with a promotion. Gifts on top of gifts, won't you say?" He shared another testimony.

Before moving, I tried everything in my powers to convince them they were making the wrong decision. I told them it's not healthy that I am being separated from my friends and grandparents with such short notice. I tried telling them it would be best to wait until I graduate from high school. I even researched some crimes that took place in the state and brought it to their attention; the power of the internet. I told them how expensive things are in New York in comparison to Memphis. Everything I tried did not work. I will say my attempts were appreciated. I saw that my parents were annoyed, yet proud of my due diligence of not giving up on something that mattered to me.

After about three months of hard attempts to persuade, I simply gave up because at that point I realized there was nothing I could have said that would have changed their minds. Let me not say give up, because I really dislike that phrase. I decided it was not worth pursuing anymore. They succeeded and I couldn't win all battles. We win some and we lose some.

However, the morning of, I gave it one last try. I told you I don't give up easily. I had locked my door for at least a good hour because I really did not want to leave. Mom and dad began trying everything they could to get me out. Nothing worked. I decided that I was not going to open that door unless they said we were staying in Memphis. Let's face it, I was desperate. If we missed the flight, it would have delayed the move. At least that was my logic.

I had planned on doing this prior, so I prepared myself. I used the bathroom, ate a big breakfast and had an extra plate hidden in my room, in case I got hungry. I even had a book in case I wanted to read because at that point everything was packed. I had my tablet and listened to music to entertain myself. I assumed pretending to play loud music while I sleep was a great alibi. A pretty good excuse if you ask me as to why I did not hear them banging and yelling through the door. Right? --- Wrong. Again, that was my logic.

My parents yelled at first, compromised, then yelled, and became concerned. I chose to remain silent through it all. They banged on the door so aggressively that it shook and then thumping sounds echoed through my bedroom. I couldn't continue on with my shenanigans. As I was about to get up to open the door, boom! My bedroom door flew open and it dangled on the hinges of the door frame, barely holding on.

I could not believe it. I was in complete shock. My mouth was open as if I had something else to say, but I didn't. We could all assume how that situation ended. As you can see, we did move to New York. However, it was not an easy journey. I put up a fight. The look on my parents' faces was filled with worry, and mom's eyes were packed with tears. They panicked, with thoughts that something had happened to me. Needless to say, what was supposed to be a joke, filled their hearts with fear. They said I would be grounded as soon as we got settled in our new home. I went too far this time. That's the story about being grounded that I mentioned earlier.

Hey, my parents did teach me to fight for a cause that I feel is worth it. For me, leaving Memphis was a reason to fight. I was leaving people who I love and care about behind.

Since we moved, mom keeps asking me if I am okay. Why ask me if you know I am not. Of course, she does it anyway, and I am honest. I always respond "I wish I was in Memphis." I am trying to get accustomed to this new place, but it is going to take time… a lot of time. The thought of starting a new school makes me so anxious, not knowing anyone and being amongst older kids. I have no idea what to expect.

I am still adjusting to a lifestyle of not being able to ride my bicycle freely because the sidewalks are so congested; being supervised during visits to Central Park because my parents are not familiar with the people in our neighborhood; living in a building and not a house; seeing different faces in the elevator, and watching different people entering and exiting their homes.

The funny thing about living in a building with others is it's often easy to know what everyone is eating for dinner. At times, I smell fish; curry something, Sazon seasoning, buttery-baked loaves of bread, and delicious fried chicken. In the mornings, when I go to empty the trash, I usually smell bacon. What's interesting is sometimes, I can tell who is cooking what on my floor.

Chapter 6
I Smell You

There is this Jamaican woman named Ms. Sandra, and whenever I smell curry, I can guess it's her cooking, and it usually is. Sometimes, I do get confused because there is another neighbor named Mr. Das from India and he cooks with a lot of curry also. Even though they both cook with curry, the smells are not exactly the same. I guess because they cook with different meats and they probably season the foods with different spices and seasonings. Nevertheless, they both smell good. Dad, being my part-time chef, says the curries come from different regions of the world, so they smell differently, and at times have different colors as well.

One day while walking back from emptying the trash, I saw Ms. Sandra in the hallway heading back to her apartment. She was carrying her mail and humming an unrecognizable song. I ask what she's cooking and she says curry goat. I'm not sure how a goat tastes curried, but it smelled spicy and inviting. Like the sushi experience, I will gladly give food from different cultures a try.

Today I saw her again as I finished emptying the trash and like before; she was carrying her mail, and this time humming a different unrecognizable song. She stopped to adjust her long grey locks. I figured I'd make conversation.

I asked, "What are you cooking that smells so divine?"

"Oxtails," she replies.

Each time I ask, I have the same indifferent expression. It smells great, but also, I have reservations if it will taste good. This time she wants to put my suspicion to an end.

"Yuh wan try som?" She speaks with her accent. Dad refers to it as Patois.

"You mean an actual ox's tail?" I am afraid to say yes but am enticed by the smell.

"Yeah. Guh ask yuh moda ef it's alright fi eat di food," she says with a smile.

I struggle to understand but translate as much of it as possible. Paying attention to keywords like mother, eat, and food, I assume she says, to ask my mom if I can have some food.

"Oh, she won't mind, she understands food is my best friend, and she likes you. She said it herself after she visited you last week." I insist, and Ms. Sandra smile showing her perfectly white and straight teeth.

Ms. Sandra laughs and invites me in and gives me a small plate. After washing my hands, I thank her and sit down to begin eating. The food is so savory; I cannot believe I am eating an ox's tail. I tell her I will be back.

"Wat happen, yuh ah guh vomit?" She says with worry.

Operative words: what happen and vomit. She's concern if I am nauseated.

"Oh no, I'm going to tell my mom where I'm at because I am coming back for a bigger plate," I say in a hurry as I excuse myself from the table.

Ms. Sandra belts out a loud boisterous laugh. She thinks I'm joking, but I am so serious. I even left her apartment door slightly cracked so I can re-enter easily. I think it's time for me to properly introduce her to the two of us; my belly and me.

What Ms. Sandra has given me is so amazing. My taste buds are tingling and feeling the excitement. The meat is so tender that with one bite, it slips off the bone and the gravy, oh my, it's heavenly and almost indescribable. My taste buds want me to hurry on back to the ox's tail.

I feel like I'm cheating on my dad's cooking. He officially has competition. It's not a fair competition because they both cook foods from different cultures. Regardless, I won't tell dad how great Ms. Sandra's food is. To him, I am his number one fan and I will continue to be. In the meantime, I run back to my apartment and ask if it's ok to go back to Ms. Sandra.

"Are you going to eat your dinner after all that food?" Mom quizzes as she types on her phone.

"Mom, come on. Do I ever say no to food? Especially when dad is cooking?"

"You are right about that. I still don't know where the food goes." She says as she makes a brief eye contact with me before locking eyes with her phone again.

"Oh, I told dad already."

"What do you mean?" She questions.

"Where the food goes?"

"And where is that?" She asks, sounding very perplexed.

"It goes to my head," I replied.

"You don't have a big head," she said placing her phone down while examining my head's circumference with intense eyes.

"Oh, I know, that's why I'm so smart. I have to feed my brain." Mom starts laughing.

"Girl, you are so silly. Tell Ms. Sandra, I said hello. What is she cooking by the way?"

"An ox's tail," I reply, assuming I know what I'm talking about.

"You mean oxtails," mom corrects me as she begins to fold up some fresh laundry.

I nod my head in a hurry to leave. I already have one foot out the door.

"Enjoy!" Mom tries to make her voice chase me.

"Little did she know, I already started to enjoy it, now I am going to finish it up."

Dad's rule in the kitchen is, whoever cooks should not do the dishes. Since dad is the one who usually cooks, mom and I are the ones who normally clean up the kitchen. The good thing is that dad usually cleans up all the while he cooks.

Having a meal prepared by him, I would clean ten kitchens. Okay, I'm lying, maybe two kitchens. Okay, okay just one. I really dislike washing plates. Mom uses this chore to her advantage when she wants to punish me or make a point. Usually, I clean up without any problems, because the kitchen is not that huge.

In that aspect of the house, dad is also adjusting to our New York, new life. Our kitchen was extremely big in our house in Memphis. However, in our new home, it's not quite as large. We do still have a dishwasher. Thank goodness! That's one of my chores, to wash the dishes along with sweeping the kitchen floor for any crumbs or food debris. Also, I am like the little cleaning lady, whose job is to wipe down the stove, counter, and dinner table, and take out the trash. Taking out the trash becomes more and more exciting, especially when I get to see Ms. Sandra. The easiest of all my chores is to load and unload the dishes from the dishwasher. It's the washing part that's annoying. So I let the dishwasher do its job and I take the credit for it.

Speaking of washing, we now use the laundry room

downstairs in our building. On Saturdays and Sundays, it is usually crowded. It's almost like everyone saves their dirty clothes for the weekends. I don't mind doing laundry. That's one chore that I do frequently. I do the entire family's laundry. Usually, every week I do three loads. One washer for color, another for whites, and the last one for delicates. Mom taught me at an early age how to use a washing machine. I'm kind of a pro now.

The delicates are usually mom's clothes. She puts most of her clothes in the dry cleaners and the others are washed in the delicate cycle. Her delicate clothes are made out of lace, satin, wool, and a few other types of fabrics. I learned this from mom, of course with her being a fashion designer and knowing a lot about different types of fabrics. She claims these particular types of materials require special care when washing.

Even though I don't mind doing laundry, I'm not too crazy about the folding aspect of it. I do it anyway because it is part of completing the entire task. When I fold the clothes, the time goes by fast because I listen to my music. I zone out and I become a folding machine. I can't say that when I work and listen to music, I get as dramatic as mom does, like when she was unpacking the dishes in our new kitchen; she imagined herself stroking the keys on an air suspended piano; she also used a spatula as a microphone. A real imagination she has.

When I asked dad why we live in an apartment building, he simply said the cost of living is different from Memphis. When I asked him what that meant, he said: "To live in New York City is very expensive. So we live in Harlem." I asked, "Why Harlem?" Oh yeah, I ask a lot of questions. Mom said it's great that I am so inquisitive.

So I asked dad "Why Harlem?"

He replied, "Because it's close to the city, but without city prices. It's within our budget. Our area is nice and quiet, and it's close to your new school. Are there any more questions?" He asks. "Nope, not for now," I reply. When I was trying to convince them not to move, I told them New York was expensive. No one listens to a kid anyway. Sometimes, they think we don't know anything, but we do.

We moved so mom can pursue her dreams of being a fashion designer and dad's job relocated him. He was given the option to relocate to one of a few other states, but he chose New York because it is the place for fashion and mom would benefit from it as well. While living in Memphis, she had a lot of customers and still has a few that request outfits to get made and shipped to them. She had turned our basement into a cute store that looked better than some clothing stores in the mall.

We had racks of colorful clothes everywhere and a few mannequins that were beautifully dressed with her creations. Customers gushed over them. She even had a cash register. I begged to be her cashier; sometimes she would let me take the money for very small-ticketed items like accessories. The larger purchases, she supervised.

Her customers always offered compliments on how good the shop looks and of course how lovely the clothes are. Mom used to say, "Even though I am making good money now, I feel like I can be making more in New York." She always felt New York City was the place to be, especially for fashion.

For her, even though she is no longer in Memphis, her customers still have access to her clothing by shopping online. The only thing is they are unable to try them on before they purchase it. I remember being in Déjà Vu, her boutique, and her customers would try on her fashions; they seemed to love everything they tried on. They came in to buy one or two pieces and ended up leaving the shop with a bag of clothes. It was great for mom because that meant that she was getting paid, but it was bad for the customers' bank accounts or their husband's credit cards.

Chapter 7
The Day Before the Big Day

We moved on August 8th, and it's now the 6th of September. I still have not made any new friends, although I have attempted to. There are a few girls in my building, who I said hi to, but they act as if I am begging them to say hello back. There are these two sisters who live on the fifth floor, and when I see them in the elevator, they always stop their entire conversation to stare at me with the meanest demeanor on their faces.

This one girl who lives on the tenth floor has a bad habit of rolling her eyes every time I see her. I have not done anything to provoke her. If anything, I'm always friendly and ready to say hello, and the moment I attempt to open my mouth, that is when her eyes begin to do this dance where it twitches first and then rolls slowly to the back of her head. It's so strange that she feels she has to do all of that. When she transforms, I simply walk away and she mumbles under her breath.

"You betta walk away. Nobody wanna be yah friend here." I

chose not to comment back because she's mumbling, and to me, that means she is not speaking directly to me, plus with her ghetto-fied English, I doubt if she understands me anyway.

When she speaks to me and acknowledges me as a person, I will give her the respect and respond back. Until then, I will continue to ignore her lips and her twitching eyes. Ugh, I hate drama.

Mom always says be careful how you treat people, because you may need them one day. I just don't understand why the twitching-eye girl and the stone-face sisters have to act the way they do. I have never done anything bad to them. I just wanted to show them I can be friendly. But like mom says, some people are just the way they are, and in some instances misery loves company, and in other cases, we just don't know what's going on in their personal lives. Mom counsels, "Baby girl, what people do and say to you has nothing to do with you. It's something that they are going through. So please, please try not to take it personally." She's ultimately right, but it's still hard to not get your feelings hurt. It's sad because I could be a really good friend to those girls, but they will never know.

My mother even caught the girl doing the eye dance to me one day; it prompted her to ask me: what was that about? I simply told mom, "I have no idea why that girl makes her face look so ugly."

"Jade, that's not nice," mom said sternly.

"I know, but mom, I did not do anything to her. Ever since the first day I saw her, her face has always been that way with me. It's almost like she trained it to do that automatically when I come around." I joked.

"Well, don't do anything to influence it or any other rude behavior from her," mom warned.

"Oh, I don't and I won't," I responded. I sure hope it won't be like this in school. Better yet, I hope those specific girls are not in my school. If they are, it will be a long and dreadful school year.

Even though I am going to a new school, it's not that different from Memphis because I would have started a new school for the sixth grade anyway. I probably would have gotten to know a few students because the community we come from is small.

Either way, I still need to make new friends, but not friends like the twitching-eye girl from downstairs. I have been so lonely these past few days. I have been bored out of my mind. I know I am the only child and I am used to not having any siblings around, but company with other girls my age would have been therapeutic. I am used to having a lot of my girlfriends around, especially Renee.

Renee and I were best friends, my entire life. We met in kindergarten and we have been inseparable, and are still inseparable, even after the move. We used to cry each other to sleep when I first moved, but now we can say goodnight over the phone without crying or getting emotional. Speaking to her is how I've been passing time these last few weeks. Mom calls us two peas in a pod; dad says we are two nuts in a tree.

Dad says all the time, "My princess is growing up fast." He always comments on how time is flying by. He adds, "Oh I remember when you were in mom's belly. I remember when I had to change your diapers. I remember when you would cry and cry for your bottle because you were hungry. You were a hungry little baby. Well, at least that much has not changed." He reaches over for a kiss on my cheek.

"Oh dad, you are always reminiscing," I remind him.

"Let me remember the good old days," he continues, "my baby is now going to middle school tomorrow."

"Dad, please don't start crying," I said teasingly.

"Jade, what are you wearing for the first day of class?" mom interrupts.

"I'm not sure yet," I reply.

"How about your hair? Are you going to leave it out or put it in a ponytail or do you want me to braid it?" Mom wants to know.

As you can see, I have a lot of hair. Sometimes it is very hard to comb. I get fed up with it often. We have a love-hate relationship. Dad says I must love and accept everything about me. Easy for him to say, he does not have to style this hair in the morning when he's half asleep.

"I will wear a ponytail as usual," I said, feeling uncertain.

Mom smoothly interjects with a solution, just as she does when some of her customers can't decide between different clothing styles or colors, "How about a ponytail? Or better yet, you know what? I can blow it out and make it straight for you. Tomorrow is a special and big day. I'll allow you to wear it straight."

"Really!" I say super excitedly. I assume my only options are a ponytail or braids. At this point, I am beyond surprised and happy.

I know it takes a lot from mom to blow out my hair just because I have so much. My hair is not only long but it is also thick. It frustrates me when I am doing it myself. When mom is blowing it out, she always says that I am giving her a real arm workout. The blow dryer is hot at times, but I rather she blows it out than to use a pressing comb.

One time my grandma tried to straighten my hair with a hot comb, I guess that's how they did it back in her days. All I remember was my scalp felt like it was on fire. Every time Grandma Hattie put that comb on my scalp it burned and I jumped and she said "Sorry baby," followed by her blowing on my traumatized scalp. It became a sequence of events each time. Again, she put the hot comb on my scalp; it burned, I jumped, and she said "Sorry baby," and blew. This went on for over an hour. When grandma was done, my hair was straighter than some girls who have a relaxer, but it didn't last long and the pain was not worth it.

When my hair is finally blown out, I fall in love with it. I can't keep my fingers out of it because it feels so soft. My mom sprays oil sheen on it to make my hair look really shiny. I absolutely love it so much that I keep swinging my head left and right; so it seems like my hair is dancing in the air.

I had a fashion show for mom with what I planned on wearing to school for the first week. I did the whole runway thing. I turned on the radio and created a runway path for her in my bedroom. The runway started at my bedroom door and ended at the window. I walked with the tempo of the music playing and tried to swing my hair with every chance I got and hitting each pose with my hand on my hip.

I even had my catwalk down really good. Mom has done several fashion shows back in Memphis. I went to most of them with dad. Some of the models would come to the house for practice and on occasions, they would teach me how to walk runway style; shoulders back, stand tall, and walk and pose and walk and pose. The only thing is for the modeling industry, I am not tall enough, but the models would always say I have time to grow. In reality, modeling is not for me. I want to be a lawyer, but in the meantime, let me satisfy mom's fashion appetite and give her the best fashion show she has ever seen.

The whole time mom was giddy like a kid in a candy store. She was so happy and jittery. She is such a sucker when it comes to fashions. She says she lives and breathes it every chance she gets. That's why every free moment she has, she is either sketching some new outfits in her book, sewing up new creations, or watching something that is fashion related on television. She works a lot of long nights now that we are more settled into our new home.

After my fashion show, she approved the outfits and I ironed them. My bookbag is lightly packed. I can't wait for tomorrow; I am beyond excited, yet a little anxious. Ok, I'm terrified. What if the girls at my new school are like the girls in my building?

Chapter 8
When It Rains, It Pours

I awake minutes before my alarm goes off, too excited to continue sleeping. I could barely sleep the night before. I'm sitting in bed, daydreaming at my clothes hanging on the outside of my wardrobe unit. Wishing I had help to dress me like Cinderella did for her ball. Unfortunately, the big ball for me is my big day in the Big Apple. I rehearsed in my head how I will greet my new classmates. I created hypothetical conversations.

"Oh yes, Memphis is lovely. Have you ever been?"

"I've been in New York City for about a month?"

"How do I like it? Ummmm, I'm adjusting."

"Nope, no brothers or sisters. Just me."

"Sweetie, are you awake?" Mom's voice interrupts my scripted hellos.

"Yes, I'm awake. You can come in." I say as I check to make

sure my hair is still protected with my scarf.

"How did you sleep?" She asks as she inspects my tired eyes and twisted head scarf.

"I didn't sleep really. I'm just a little nervous, that's all." My nervousness shows as I struggle to straighten the sheets properly, while making my bed.

"You will be ok. I've heard great things about your homeroom teacher Mrs. Bailey. I spoke with her personally and she's aware you're transferring from a different state," mom says with care and assurance.

"Mom, I don't want special privileges. Why did you do that?" I briefly snap at the situation.

"I'm just trying to help. You should be ok," she reassures.

"Great, so now I will be placed under a microscope, right?" I question.

"Jade, relax. You will be ok. Ok?" She offers a smile of encouragement.

"Dad already left for work but left you a note. You can read it as you eat your cereal," she says shifting topics.

'Sweetie, sorry I'm not there to take you to school. I'm sure you will have an amazing day. Remember how incredible you are. Remember how beautiful you are and how rare. I love you, my gem.'

I put the bowl to my head and slurp the remaining milk and I grab the note and head to my room to get ready.

Minutes later, I am dressed. My new denim jeans fit perfectly. I pair them with a graphic tee that matches the seven colors in my new sneakers. The very last thing to do is to comb out my hair. Mom wrapped it in a doobie last night to keep it straight. Her focus on making my center part straight took forever. So I comb my velvety soft hair to flow in the direction of the part that bounces with every movement I make.

"Jade, are you ready?" mom yells from the living room.

"Yes, I'm coming now," as I grab my bookbag. I pause for a second in the mirror to admire myself and dance my way back to the front door.

"You have everything? Do you need a jacket just in case the school is cold from the AC? Oh, make sure you grab that umbrella. There's supposed to be scattered showers today," she says as she pointed to my umbrella on the coffee table.

"Oh, I forgot! I gotta get dad's letter," I say as I'm running back to my room causing me to dismiss everything she said.

"Hurry, we have to go now," her voice trails me as I head to my room.

I quickly grab the note and place it in my back pocket and run out the door that mom is holding with her back leaned against it, as she texts on her phone.

On our ride to school, mom seems just as distracted and anxious as I am. We both have a big day ahead of us. After dropping me off, she will head to a very important business meeting. She is professionally dressed in a black pencil skirt with a floral blouse. Her red lipstick matches the rose print in her shirt perfectly.

"We are about ten minutes from the school. Are you feeling less nervous?" She asks while talking over the news on the radio.

"I'm more excited than anything now," I reply.

"Oh great! Your hair looks fabulous, by the way," she says as she observes me in her rearview mirror.

"Yeah, thanks," I say as I play with the zipper from my bookbag, which was fairly old. Mom wanted to get me a new one, but I insisted on keeping it.

"Jaaaade," mom says with a brief silence, and then followed

by, "did you grab the umbrella from the coffee table?" she says with panic in her voice.

I look out the window and up at the sky that is suddenly dark grey. Within minutes, speckles of raindrops land on the window. I grab my silky smooth hair and gasp.

"Oh nooo... Mom, I forgot it. We have to go back." I say, ringing an alarm.

"Sweetie, we can't. You will be late on your first day and I cannot be late for this meeting either," she says with her eyes fixed on the road.

"But mom! My hair! What about my hair?" a crisis is in full effect.

"Jade, you will be ok." Silence fills the car and we both listen to a full-fledged thunderstorm. The rain slams on the car windows, hood and trunk. It's now a complete downpour. The windshield wipers are moving at its fastest speed but still cannot keep up with the showers.

"Nooooo, what am I supposed to do now?" I say, as mom parks behind a line of about six vehicles of parents dropping off their children.

Her eyes glance at her watch as she adjusts the hair in her face and exhales her own hidden emotions.

What am I to do? If rain gets on my hair, it will transform instantly. I'm fine with my natural hair, I actually love it. However, I do have a hair regimen that I do the night before to get my curls to coil and for it to have a certain bounce and look. The rain will make me look like a wet poodle.

I scan the entire car to find something, anything I could use as a makeshift umbrella. Nothing, absolutely nothing is available.

"Is there anything in the trunk I can use to cover with?" I ask desperately.

"Sorry sweetie, no, just the first-aid kit." How I wish someone would come to my aide. Mom is usually the queen of options. Today she came up short, like the star player on the team missing an open layup.

"Fine, I'll just run for it and put my book bag over my head," I say with defeat in my voice, but refusing to allow rain to mess up this big day.

I stare out the window at the ground and it's drenched. Puddles have already formed between the cracks and crevices on the pavement. The car begins to move again and comes to a quick halt. Still, there is a fleet of cars filled with children trying to maintain shelter through the storm. One by one, the brave ones hop out of the car and make a dash to the entrance of the school. Some have umbrellas, some shield themselves with their jackets and others use my book bag idea. Needless to say, they are all running to avoid feeling the tears the sky is crying.

It is now my turn to endure the storm. Mom pulls up and parks the car. I analyze the distance and it seems like I will have to run half-court, from the car to the front entrance of the school. I unfasten my seatbelt and am about to take off and she says,

"Emmmm, where's my sugar young lady?" mom points to her cheeks.

"Mom, I'm in a crisis right now." I lean forward to give her a kiss on the cheek.

"Thank you. Now, on your mark, get set, go!" she directs me.

I run out of the car with my bookbag attempting to cover me. Fortunately, the rain is not as heavy at the moment, which makes it easier to run. The wind slaps my face and instantly, strands of what used to be straight and silky hair are now curled up and plastered on my cheek. My exposed arms are completely wet and my colorful graphic tee is damp and now the rainbow-like colors don't look as vibrant.

I look ahead and see that my journey is halfway complete. I

release a hard exhale and begin to run harder and faster as if I have to break the tape at the end of a race.

"Jade! Jade!" mom yells at me as the wind and rain muffles her normal speaking voice.

I turn around to see her running toward me. Papers are dancing in the air with the wind. Some are sealed to the ground. Confused as to what is happening, I see my purple pencil case on the ground, I then realize my bookbag is open and everything has escaped. I must not have zippered up my bag when I was playing with the zipper moments ago.

Mom and I fumble to catch the flying papers; we even peel a few sheets off the wet ground, which is difficult. My bare nails scrape the wet pavement. At this point, my bag is no longer a shield and my belongings are drenched.

After what feels like forever, we finally gather all my things and make it inside the dry yet cold air-conditioned school. I am in a complete daze, yet still, alert thanks to the goose bumps that have formed due to the frigid air in the school. This all seems surreal. Mom wipes the remaining raindrops from my face and brings me back to reality.

"How unbelievable is that?" Mom says as she attempts to organize my clammy school papers. What's more unbelievable is how beautiful mom still looks although the rain is scattered all over her.

"I really want to go home, this can't be my first day," I say, observing my disheveled self.

"Honey, it's not as bad as you think," she says, trying to convince me.

"Excuse me, Ma'am! Excuse me! You have to move your vehicle. It's delaying the drop off line for other parents," says a heavyset, balding man dressed as a security officer.

"Please give me five minutes, while I get my child situated," mom pleads.

"Ma'am, we already gave you five minutes. I'm afraid if you don't return soon, you will get ticketed," he advises.

"Excuse me, what's your name," she demands.

"Officer Wallace is my name. Do as you see fit with it," He says in a condescending tone and chuckles as he goes back outside to take on another mother; this time with Mother Nature.

"Honey, what else do you need?" she asks looking more concerned than ever.

"To go home, but I know that's not an option. So nothing. I will be alright." I tap my back pocket to make sure my dad's love note is still tucked away. I will read it in a few minutes to calm my nerves.

"Come, let me put your hair in a braid or something," she says and beckons for me to come closer.

Mom attempts to make a big French braid. I feel her struggle. We both know that a brush, comb and hair products are needed. Mom uses her fingers to comb my hair. She steps back and takes a look at me from head to toe. She hesitates and walks back to me. She then takes the braid out, fluffs my hair, and continues to comb it with her delicate fingers.

"Ok sweetie, you're good to go," she says with very little confidence. We both know this was one of her rare white lies.

I stand there being examined by her. Children enter the building one by one with no traces of rain. It must have stopped. Great, so it pours just for me, huh!

"Do you remember your homeroom teacher's name?" Mom quizzes.

"Yes, it's Mrs. Bailey," I figure since she will be my teacher for a year, I should remember her name.

"Ok great. Head to class and I will see you later. Try to have a great day; don't let this morning set the tone. You have the power to make it a better day." She preaches.

I walk away looking for my homeroom number and teacher's name to match. I choose not to look back and allow my eyes to follow her to the exit, to where I wish I was going as well. As I continue to walk, I felt something hit me, but when I looked on the floor, I didn't see anything that could have bounced off of me.

"Aye, puff puff, you dropped your pencil case outside," explains, a tall Hispanic girl with very long wavy hair. She holds my purple pencil case out for me to reach and get it. The closer she gets, the more she towers over me and allows me to see her features even more. She's gorgeous and is even wearing makeup. She is built like an eighth grader or even someone who belongs in high school. I'm immediately intimidated, but I try to conceal it.

"Ohh thanks," I smile big and bright, hoping she could be a new friend.

As our hands almost meet, I notice her freshly polished hot pink nails. Then suddenly her hand releases its grip and purposely drops my pencil case, and she walks away laughing with her friends. I even heard her say "You saw that big mole on her cheek? Holy Moly!" They all laugh in unison as I pick up my pencils that fell out of its case. Lifting myself up off the cold floor, I see her and her clique walking back. I stand up immediately.

"Aye, puff puff!" She intensely stares at me from a distance searching for weakness. Like a lioness to its prey, I keep my face emotionless, shoulders back, head high, making direct eye contact, and showing no fear.

"You missed one," she says.

My eyes glance across the floor. I see nothing.

"It's in your hair, holy moly. See you later." She tries to torment me; she laughs and walks away again to her waiting clique of friends.

A few other students walk by laughing, staring, and snickering. I am beyond mortified, mainly because I am alone for all of this.

I start to search for the pencil that was supposedly aimed at my hair like an arrow hitting its intended target. My hands circle my hair, blindly feeling around for it.

"Let me help, are you ok?" A friendly voice asks.

"Yeah, are you alright? Marisol is the meanest." Another pleasant yet serious voice says with true concern.

I turn around and I am greeted by a warm yet pitying smile from the stone-faced sisters from my building.

Let's Have a Chat

Hi parents, family members, and readers,

Here are a few questions that I think might create new conversations. Feel free to discuss amongst yourself and if you feel comfortable send the responses to Julieann at FindingTheJEMS@gmail.com. I would love to hear from you!

Can you relate to the main character, Jade?

Have you ever been on a plane? If so, what was it like? If not, where would you like to go?

What is the most adventurous food you have tried? And did you enjoy it?

Is it easy to make new friends?

Have you experienced any kind of unfairness and bullying?

What will happen in book two with Jade and the stone-faced sisters?

Do you think Marisol will become an issue for Jade?

Please email any other questions you may have to FindingTheJEMS@gmail.com.

Continue to find the gems in life.
With my highest gratitude,
Julieann T. Randall

Excited? Read More!!

Be Sure to Get Book Two

Jade's Journey

Sign up at www.findingthejems.com/contact to receive the latest news and exclusive offers.

FINDING THE JEMS
DISCOVERY THROUGH LITERACY

Vocabulary Builder

- Carnivore
- Circumference
- Discombobulated
- Due diligence
- Ecstatic
- Furrow
- Hypothetical
- Immaculate
- Indescribable
- Inquisitive
- Intimidate
- Miraculous

- Misconstrue
- Monologue
- Mortified
- Nonchalant
- Oxymoronic
- Patronize
- Psuedo
- Shenanigans
- Simultaneous
- Synchronize
- Traumatize
- Torment

FINDING THE JEMS
DISCOVERY THROUGH LITERACY

Discover the Meaning

Carnivore *noun* car·ni·vore
: a meat eater — sometimes used humorously to refer to
people who eat meat
Sentence: I love my protein, hence, the nicknames
meatatarian or carnivore.

Circumference *noun* cir·cum·fer·ence
: the outer edge of a shape or area
Sentence: "You don't have a big head," she said placing her
phone down while examining my head's circumference with
intense eyes.

Discombobulated *verb* dis·com·bob·u·late
: thrown into confusion
Sentence: Her face looks even more discombobulated.

Diligence *noun* dil·i·gence
: careful and continued hard work
Sentence: I saw that my parents were annoyed, yet proud of
me doing my due diligence and not giving up on something
that mattered to me.

Ecstatic *adjective* ec·stat·ic
: very happy or excited: feeling or showing ecstasy
Sentence: Mom says ecstatically as her voice pierces my eardrums.

Furrow *noun* fur·row
: a narrow line or wrinkle in the skin of a person's face
Sentence: Her eyebrows furrow in the center of her forehead.

Hypothetical *adjective* hy·po·thet·i·cal
: not real: imagined as an example
Sentence: I created hypothetical conversations.

Immaculate *adjective* im·mac·u·late
: perfectly clean
Sentence: That was a close call considering mom and I just swept and mopped our immaculate floors.

Indescribable *adjective* in·de·scrib·a·ble
: impossible to describe: very great or extreme
Sentence: The meat is so tender that with one bite, it slips off the bone and the gravy, oh my, it's heavenly and almost indescribable.

Inquisitive *adjective* in·quis·i·tive
: tending to ask questions: having a desire to know or learn more
Sentence: I said with my most inquisitive voice.

Intimidate *verb* in·tim·i·date
: to make (someone) afraid
Sentence: I'm immediately intimidated, but I try to conceal it.

Miraculous *adjective* mi·rac·u·lous
: very wonderful or amazing like a miracle
Sentence: The ambiance of the lobby is absolutely beautiful

and it's miraculously changing my mood by filling me up with positive energy.

Misconstrue _verb_ mis·con·strue
: to understand (something) incorrectly
Sentence: She completely misconstrued my seriousness as silliness.

Monologue _noun_ mono·logue
: a long speech made by one person that prevents anyone else from talking
Sentence: Instead, I edit my monologue, my tone, and facial expression.

Mortified _verb_ mor·ti·fy
: to cause (someone) to feel very embarrassed and foolish
Sentence: I am beyond mortified, mainly because I am alone for all of this.

Nonchalant _adjective_ non·cha·lant
: relaxed and calm in a way that shows that you do not care or are not worried about anything
Sentence: Dad is baffled by the mess and my nonchalant tone.

Oxymoronic _noun_ ox·y·mo·ron
: a combination of words that have opposite or very different meanings
Sentence: We are in the heart of an oxymoronic rush hour.

Patronize _verb_ pa·tron·ize
: to talk to (someone) in a way that shows that you believe you are more intelligent than other people
Sentence: Patronizing him as I slowly creep toward the kitchen.

Pseudo *adjective* pseu·do
: not real or genuine: FAKE
Sentence: I have something to look forward to after this pseudo cleanup.

Shenanigans *noun* she·nan·i·gan
: activity or behavior that is not honest or proper
Sentence: I couldn't continue on with my shenanigans.

Simultaneous *adjective* si·mul·ta·ne·ous
: happening at the same time
Sentence: My eyes scan the insides of the fridge, using his cues to quickly reach for it as I simultaneously ask myself.

Synchronize *verb* syn·chro·nize
: to happen at the same time and speed
Sentence: She swings her hips from side to side, synchronizing to the beat.

Traumatize *verb* trau·ma·tize
: to cause (someone) to become very upset in a way that often leads to serious emotional problems
Sentence: "Sorry baby," followed by her blowing on my traumatized scalp.

Torment *noun* tor·ment
: extreme physical or mental pain
Sentence: She tries to torment me; she laughs and walks away again to her waiting clique of friends.

Discover Words with Jade

```
R  F  Y  C  Q  S  T  R  A  G  J  F  C  J  O  W  P  Q  P  Z
E  V  D  S  T  U  A  K  V  A  F  D  X  K  A  E  J  O  E  O
H  V  T  W  M  V  R  Y  H  P  V  I  Q  T  Y  T  W  D  L  N
X  L  I  H  X  Q  F  U  R  W  A  R  E  M  C  A  E  K  P  I
L  I  E  T  Q  N  W  U  A  M  I  R  A  C  U  L  O  U  S  I
L  Y  T  P  I  Z  D  P  D  L  P  Z  B  I  W  U  F  D  X  J
S  J  V  J  O  S  P  S  Y  N  Z  G  R  A  K  B  X  W  G  U
X  J  E  E  G  W  I  E  Z  P  H  F  X  Q  O  O  Z  L  D  O
Q  W  U  D  C  F  A  U  J  J  R  D  E  N  L  B  A  U  E  D
B  G  R  B  J  X  R  G  Q  N  L  R  K  Z  L  M  C  Y  R  U
K  J  T  L  W  K  U  O  R  N  O  K  Z  B  F  O  E  O  J  E
S  M  S  Y  N  S  I  L  T  V  I  M  S  H  X  C  Y  X  G  S
P  C  N  Q  K  Y  M  O  I  V  L  O  W  A  W  S  D  Y  Y  P
B  I  O  G  I  J  S  N  R  B  P  O  H  O  A  I  I  M  J  J
T  T  C  I  K  Z  R  O  Y  T  R  N  T  W  O  D  P  O  O  K
L  A  S  Z  U  A  L  M  L  R  Y  H  G  L  Q  U  E  R  G  D
V  T  I  V  C  P  K  A  U  E  J  X  L  J  I  X  R  O  Y  J
R  S  M  G  H  B  H  F  A  F  X  E  V  B  D  I  N  N  J  V
V  C  J  H  J  Z  J  D  Z  N  N  L  W  A  A  Z  G  I  N  X
L  E  Y  U  B  J  Q  X  D  R  O  W  U  S  S  Y  R  C  P  D
```

INQUISITIVE

ECSTATIC

DISCOMBOBULATE

MIRACULOUS

MISCONSTRUE

OXYMORONIC

MONOLOGUE

FURROW

PSEUDO

CARNIVORE

68

Build Words with Jade

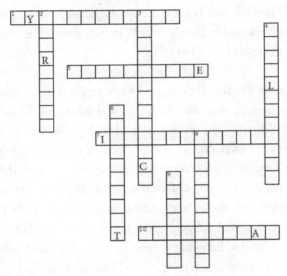

Down

2. To treat in a snobbish manner.
3. The boundary line of a figure, area, or object.
4. Happening, existing, or done at the same time.
6. Seeming to be coolly unconcerned or indifferent.
8. To make timid; fill with fear.
9. To cause to experience shame, humiliation, or wounded pride; humiliate.

Across

1. Uncertain; conditional
5. Impeccably clean; spotless.
7. Impossible to describe
10. A playful or mischievous act; a prank.

Bonus Word _____

Unscramble letters given Y A R L E T C I

69

About the Author

Julieann T. Randall was born in Kingston, Jamaica, raised in the Bronx, New York and currently resides in New Jersey. She obtained her degree through CUNY, City College.

As a passionate literacy advocate and youth empowerment speaker, Julieann created Finding the JEMS (Joint Educational Movement Soldiers) to shine a light on literacy and make reading a priority. Forming an army of relentless soldiers focused on higher education to support literacy development, Julieann sees it as her duty to introduce underprivileged children to their right to literacy by exposing them to books and educational programs they are normally not awarded. Julieann, also known as Jules often refers to children as gems. Reminding them how precious and valuable they are. She plans to reach many more children from the US. and other parts of the world through her books, future book drives, and educational programs.

CPSIA information can be obtained
at www.ICGtesting.com
Printed in the USA
FFHW010007080319
50859181-56259FF